TOAD
ATTACK!

TOAD ATTACK!

PATRICE LAWRENCE

With illustrations by
Becka Moor

Barrington Stoke

First published in 2019 in Great Britain by
Barrington Stoke Ltd
18 Walker Street, Edinburgh, EH3 7LP

www.barringtonstoke.co.uk

Text © 2019 Patrice Lawrence
Illustrations © 2019 Becka Moor

A CIP catalogue record for this book is available
from the British Library upon request

ISBN: 978-1-78112-844-2

Printed in China by Leo

To Aliya, for the inspiration!

CONTENTS

Chapter 1

A Toad on the Head

On Wednesday morning, Leo Hogg stepped out
of his house and was hit on the head by a toad.
It bounced off, slid down his nose and landed
on his left shoe. Leo's small brown eyes stared
into the toad's big red ones. Leo blinked. So
did the toad. Then the toad flicked out its
tongue, pushed down on Leo's foot and flew up
onto the low branch of a nearby tree. It hopped
higher and higher until it was balancing on
a thick twig at the top. A breeze ruffled the
leaves. The toad wobbled, then fell, but instead
of landing in a splat at Leo's feet, it caught a

1

gust of wind and flew up and over Leo's roof until it was gone.

"Leo?" Granddad was by the front door. "Have you forgotten something?"

"No, Granddad, it's just ..." Leo looked up at his roof. A pigeon was sitting on the satellite dish and looking down at the road as if it owned it. There were no toads anywhere. Had Leo dreamed the flying toad? "It's nothing, Granddad," he said.

"Hurry up, then! Oh, and can you come by the workshop on your way home? I need you to help me fix Lisa Tank's golf brolly. That umbrella needs a lot of work."

"Can't Mum help?" Leo asked.

"She's busy working on a new type of tornado umbrella. Even the strongest winds won't turn it inside out."

"We don't have many tornadoes in Upper Dab, Granddad."

Granddad smiled. "True. But they do in other places. Your mum reckons that these will be her best brollies ever."

Leo smiled back at Granddad. "Like the umbrellas that could turn into cat beds?"

"Don't be cheeky, Leo. I think your mum's on to something this time. One day, we'll have a real umbrella shop again."

A noisy crowd of Upper Dab High School students were waiting for the bus opposite Leo's house. It was funny to think that Leo would be heading to secondary school next year. Would he ever be as tall as them? They were too busy chatting to see what was on the litter bin next to them. It was another toad, pale yellow like the last. It leaped up, legs springing out like party poppers behind it. It landed on top of the bus-stop sign. Leo's heart

was thumping hard. He hadn't imagined it.
Toads could fly. He'd never seen that before.

His phone buzzed in his pocket. Leo took it
out and checked it. It was a text from his best
friend, Rosa:

Get here quick, Leo!

He texted back:

I'm walking as quick as I can!

She replied straight away:

Run, Leo! Run!

Why?

You'll see!

He shoved his phone deep into his pocket
and crossed the road to Dab Deals industrial
estate. He tightened the straps of his rucksack,
took a deep breath and RAN! He sprinted

through the empty car park, jumped over the small fence by Bug In A Rug carpet shop and tore through Clackers housing estate. He staggered out onto Dab Drive and through the school gates.

Rosa had already arrived at Dab Juniors and was sitting on the wall by the nature garden. The gate was open and Leo could see Mr Pringle, the head teacher, watering the flowerbeds and pots.

"What took you so long?" Rosa said.

Leo took off his rucksack and flopped down next to her. "Something really odd happened."

Rosa held up her phone to show him. "Something odd like this?"

Chapter 2

A Toad Called Twerky

Leo squinted at the picture on Rosa's phone screen. She was in her garden with her hand held out. A big toad sat in the middle of her palm.

She grinned at Leo. "It's not just any toad. It's a flying toad! Dad Raj is so excited!"

Dad Raj would be excited. He was the main presenter on the *Warts and All* TV nature programme.

"I saw one too," Leo said. "I thought I was imagining it at first."

"Me too!" Rosa said. "I saw it from the kitchen. It looked like it jumped off our fig tree and, well, just started to fly." Rosa's eyes shone with excitement. "Dad Raj caught it while it was munching on a slug. I've called it Twerky."

Leo raised his eyebrows. "Twerky?"

"Yes!" Rosa signed the letters – T W E R K Y – slowly, to annoy him. She knew Leo had spent all summer practising British Sign Language. She'd been the one teaching him. Rosa could hear a little with her hearing aids. She was also very good at lip-reading, but British Sign Language was great for making secret plans.

"I understood you the first time," he said. "It's just that Twerky's a funny name for a toad."

"It's a funny type of toad," Rosa said. "And when it's breathing, its bottom sort of moves, as if it's twerking – so, Twerky!"

Leo laughed. "Are you keeping Twerky as a pet?"

Rosa shook her head. "Dad Raj wants to examine it and let it go. It's not every day that a flying toad lands in your garden."

"Does he know where they came from?" Leo asked.

"No, but he's trying to find out. He's making a special *Warts and All* programme about them."

As they sat chatting, the nature-garden gate opened wider. Plum Pringle, the head's

daughter, came out. She had a small wicker cat basket in her arms.

"Plum!" Mr Pringle ran out after her. "Bring her back! We still need her! There's a fat slug on the bean plant."

Plum spotted Leo and Rosa. She held the cat basket closer to her and ran back into the nature garden. The gate closed.

Rosa nudged Leo. "Wow! Mr Pringle's even trained his cat to help with the garden."

"I'm not surprised," Leo said. "If we don't win Dab's Best Blooms this year, he's going to explode."

"Yeah!" Rosa laughed. "Did you see his face when Nae Nae Juniors beat us last year? He looked like he was going to explode then."

They put their phones away and headed into school.

Chapter 3

Toads of Terror

After lunch, Leo's teacher, Miss Quaver, led the class out into the nature garden. Mr Pringle and the gardening club were making a great job of it. Maybe this year they had a real chance of winning Dab's Best Blooms. Pots of tomatoes and blackcurrants stood against a wall that had been painted a pale sky blue with clouds. The reception class had made pom-pom birds that dangled from a tiny apple tree. Bean plants trailed up canes. Bees hummed around a bush of pink roses and clumps of spikey lavender. Leo breathed in the flowery perfume.

"OK," Miss Quaver said. "As you know, the judges are visiting us on Saturday. Mr Pringle has asked for your help. We're not allowed to use any slug pellets or other poison, so pests have to be removed by hand."

Miss Quaver split them into groups. She gave each group a bucket and gardening gloves and told them to collect any snails or slugs they found in the garden. They were allowed to squash greenfly and squirt special soapy water over blackfly. One group had to check leaves for butterfly eggs.

"Hungry caterpillars will munch through this whole garden in no time," Miss Quaver said.

Rosa picked a snail out of a tomato plant and dropped it into her bucket. "This is my kind of lesson!" she said.

Suddenly a voice boomed, "Excuse me, Miss Quaver! I'm afraid there's been a change of plan!"

Mr Pringle came into the garden followed by a woman with a camera on her shoulder and a sound man with a big fluffy microphone.

Leo tapped Rosa on the shoulder. "Look! We're going to be famous!"

Mr Pringle went over to talk to Miss Quaver. She nodded but didn't look happy.

"Sorry, class," she said. "Mr Pringle needs the garden for an interview."

Everybody groaned, took off their gloves and handed back the buckets. Just as Leo passed Mr Pringle, he saw the camera woman take a big rubber toad out of her rucksack.

She said, "We don't have any real toads to show our viewers. We will have to use this."

She put the toad on Mr Pringle's shoulder. He looked very unhappy indeed.

She said, "Thank you for letting us into your wonderful garden, Mr Pringle. There are only two more days until the winner of Dab's Best Blooms is chosen. Do you think you'll win this year?"

Mr Pringle puffed himself up. "Of course we'll win! Our garden is the best it's ever been."

The camera woman nodded. "I've heard that some very unusual toads have been spotted in Upper Dab, Mr Pringle. These are very hungry toads that seem to be able to fly. Will your garden be safe?"

Then Miss Quaver called Leo over, so he didn't have a chance to hear how Mr Pringle replied.

*

After school, Leo walked back with Rosa.

She said, "Dad Raj texted me to say he's going to be late tonight as he's doing loads of interviews about the toads. They're turning up all over town."

"Flying toads in Upper Dab! He must be delighted," Leo said.

"He's worried," Rosa said. "Toads shouldn't just drop out of the sky." She took out her phone and clicked on a film. "He sent me this."

A squashy-faced cat was lying across the bonnet of a car. Three toads dropped down from a nearby tree and landed next to it. The cat stood up, arched its back and slapped the smallest toad off the car. The two bigger toads hopped closer to the cat. Their tongues shot out and slapped the cat's ear. The cat jumped to its feet, fur on end, and shot off the car. It then ran down the street as the toads bounced and glided behind it.

"Poor Nigel," Rosa said.

"Who's Nigel?" asked Leo.

"The cat's called Nigel," said Rosa. She clicked another link. A woman had posted a selfie with the cat. A caption underneath shouted "TOADS OF TERROR!"

"She's Mary Grimbow. Nigel's her cat. He was terrified," Rosa explained.

"He must have seen himself in a mirror," Leo said. "He's a funny-looking cat."

Rosa's face stayed serious. "Nigel can't help how he looks." She popped her phone back into her bag. "Toads should be scared of cats, Leo. Something really weird is happening."

*

Leo left Rosa at the end of Dab Drive and carried on to the Dolly's Brollies workshop. It wasn't really a workshop any more. It was more of a work corner, stuck at the back of a shoe shop. When Leo was little, his grandma, Dolly, had owned the shop. Then the shop sold umbrellas and his grandma ran the shop at the front, while Granddad fixed old umbrellas and designed new ones in the workshop at the back. Leo loved that shop. He loved looking at the racks of umbrellas, counting the different colours and choosing his favourite, hoping each week that they wouldn't be sold. As he got older, his favourites stayed in the shop longer and longer until nobody seemed to buy any umbrellas at all. When Grandma died, the shop closed. Maria, the new owner, turned it into a shoe shop. Mum and Granddad helped out with shoe repairs round the back, as well as keeping a corner for their brollies, but they still dreamed about having a real umbrella shop again.

The little bell above the shop door rang as Leo went in. Maria was behind the counter, staring at her phone. She looked up.

"Is this your school on the news, Leo?"

He nodded.

"And there's really a swarm of flying toads?"

"I think so."

"Is that why Mr Pringle's got a toad on his shoulder?"

Leo nodded again.

"He doesn't look very happy about it."
Maria picked up a shoe and stroked the leather.
"Toad skin. I wonder how tough it is." She saw
the look on Leo's face and put the shoe back
down. "Just joking."

Leo went through the door behind the
counter, past the high shelves stacked with
boxes of shoes and boots. Normally, everything
was quiet back here. Granddad would be
sewing on a shoe buckle and Mum fixing a hole
in a shoe sole. No one would be talking. Today,
Leo could hear them before he saw them.

"What about this, Angela?" Granddad
sounded excited.

"Yes!" Mum said. "It comes in so many colours. We can match them to Maria's shoes and put them in the shop window."

Granddad clapped. "Great idea!"

Leo peered round the shelves. "Mum? Granddad?"

They were side by side looking at the pictures in a big book. Leo could see little scraps of fabric pinned to the pages.

Mum looked up. "Toads, Leo!"

"And they're flying!" Granddad waved his arms around. "Flying! Do you know what that means?"

"They can fly?" said Leo.

Mum and Granddad rolled their eyes at the same time.

Mum said, "When toads go up, what comes down?"

"Toads?"

"Precisely!" Mum agreed. "People have been filming them and putting it online. The toads don't exactly fly. They sort of glide and drop. One just missed Sally Sparkle when she was out for her lunch-time jog." Mum held up the skeleton of a big umbrella. "Our tornado umbrellas are perfect. They stop toads plopping down on people's heads."

"What if the toads are only plopping down in Upper Dab?" Leo said.

Another double eye roll.

"The toads can glide for miles." Granddad said it slowly, trying to make Leo understand. "They must have come from somewhere. So why can't they glide somewhere else? To another town, across the sea, maybe around the world." He tapped a half-made umbrella on the floor. "And Dolly's Brollies will be ready with our Toad-Busters. Before you know it, we'll have a proper shop again."

"Maybe two shops," Mum said.

Granddad frowned. "Just two, Angela? Two hundred! We'll have shops around the world!"

Leo backed away. "I'll leave you to it."

Chapter 4

Monster Toads

Next morning, a text arrived from Rosa as Leo was eating his cornflakes.

Dad Raj is on Frosty Morning!

Leo switched on the television. "Granddad! It's Rosa's Dad Raj!"

Dad Raj was sitting on the sofa opposite the presenter, Esi Frost. A cross-looking woman with a funny-looking cat on her lap sat next to him.

"It's Nigel!" Leo yelled.

Granddad squinted at the screen. "No, I think that's Mary Grimbow. She runs the flower shop near the station."

"No! Her cat's called Nigel!" Leo explained. "The toads chased him down the road."

"Ah, yes." Granddad took a slurp of his tea. "They all ganged up on him, didn't they?"

Dad Raj was leaning towards Esi Frost. She was nodding like she agreed with every word he was saying. Leo turned up the volume.

"We still aren't sure where these toads came from," Dad Raj was saying. "But we think they're related to cane toads."

"Cane toads!" Mary Grimbow lurched forwards. Nigel yowled in protest. "They eat everything in their path! They're monsters! And these ones fly."

Dad Raj gave her a friendly smile. "We just *think* they're related. We don't know for sure. But what we do know is that there are far fewer toads in the world than there should be. Every time we use slug pellets in our gardens, we kill more toads. Every time we destroy ponds and marshes to build roads and houses, we kill more toads. We should be happy that this new breed has chosen Upper Dab as its home."

Esi Frost looked into the camera. "Should we be happy? Call us now and let us know what you think." She reached under her desk and brought out a fish tank. The camera zoomed in on the toad inside. Leo guessed that it was Twerky. "Friend or foe?" asked Esi Frost.

A scream cut the air. The camera swung towards Mary Grimbow, who was rubbing a scratch mark on her hand. Nigel streaked away from the sofa and out of sight.

"Take that thing away!" Mary Grimbow shouted at Esi Frost. "It's scaring my Nigel!"

She jumped off the sofa and followed the cat. "Nigel! It's OK, sweetie. You're safe."

The TV channel cut to the adverts.

Rosa was waiting on the wall by the nature garden. Leo sat down next to her.

"I counted twelve toads on my way in," he said.

Rosa said, "I counted eleven."

"Does Dad Raj really think they're a good thing?"

She shrugged. "Some toad experts came over to our house last night to examine Twerky. They took loads of pictures and a tiny bit of his blood to test. If he is a cane toad, there's going to be all sorts of problems. Cane toads really do eat everything in their path, including other toads' eggs. These ones can get up into trees and birds' nests. Nothing will be safe."

Leo thought of Mum and Granddad, planning their toad-proof umbrellas.

He said, "Maybe they could be good for Upper Dab."

The bell rang and they stood up. "I hope so," Rosa said.

The nature garden gate opened. Plum Pringle came out. She was carrying the cat basket again. Mr Pringle was right behind her.

"Plum!" he called. "Don't take her away yet! We haven't finished!"

Leo and Rosa looked at each other.

Rosa said, "That must be one very hungry cat."

Suddenly Rosa frowned and rubbed her hearing aid. "Was that a really loud noise or have my hearing aids gone funny?"

Leo said, "It was a really loud noise!"

It sounded like a sad trombone and it seemed to be coming from Plum Pringle's cat.

Leo said, "Look over there, Rosa!"

A pair of toads was bouncing across the playground towards Plum. A third toad dropped from the windowsill by the boys' toilets and landed at Plum's feet. Another toad came and another one, all plopping to the ground and looking up at her.

Another sad trombone toot came from the basket.

Rosa said, "That's a really strange cat in there."

The toads by Plum's feet sucked in their bodies and opened their mouths. The noise they made was like a ship's horn blasted through the biggest megaphone in the world. The playground went silent and everyone watched as an extra-big toad jumped up onto

the wall where Leo and Rosa had been sitting.
The toad's wide mouth seemed to be grinning
at Plum.

"Dad," Plum said in a tiny voice. "Do
something."

Mr Pringle just stood there. His eyes were popping out more than those of the toads.

"I don't know what to do," he said.

The school bell blasted through the outside speakers. The toads pushed down on their front legs and launched into the air. Plum ran back into the nature garden. Mr Pringle followed her, calling her name.

"This isn't going to be a normal Thursday, is it?" Leo said.

*

After Miss Quaver had taken the register, it was time for assembly. Leo sat with the other Year 6s on the benches at the back, while Rosa was at the front to see the British Sign Language interpreter better. Mr Pringle stood on the stage with the teachers sitting on chairs behind him.

He said, "Only two days to go before the Dab's Best Blooms judges come and visit our wonderful little garden." He rubbed his hands together. "And this year I am happy to say that we have the best chance of winning, ever."

Leo watched the interpreter sign "best". Rosa looked back at Leo and rolled her eyes.

Mr Pringle turned to the white screen behind him and said, "Let's remind ourselves who we're up against."

A picture of a garden flashed up. The caption said "Krump Middle School". It looked perfectly fine to Leo. There was a giant cactus and a bush with some bright yellow flowers and a basket with strawberries hanging out of it.

Mr Pringle smiled. "They haven't won for three years and I don't think they will this year, either."

Next up was the Slide Music School. Leo liked this one better. Flowers sprouted out of a trombone, ivy trailed out of a trumpet and they'd planted cress in a violin case.

Slide's garden disappeared and a new picture took its place.

"And this is the offering from Nae Nae Juniors, last year's winners," said Mr Pringle.

The whole hall went "Wow!" – even the teachers. Mr Pringle glared out at everyone. There were beds of white and pink flowers, and pots with lemon trees and fig trees. An old bath tub was filled with plants trailing bright orange and yellow flowers. Little wooden markers poked between the leaves said "Cucumbers" and "Marrows". In the middle of the garden was a tower made from bricks, logs and hollow pipes. A banner draped across the top said "Nae Nae Juniors Bug Hotel". Tiny signs were stuck on to different parts of the hotel. There were Ladybird Bedrooms and a Wormy Basement and an Ant Gym and—

"Mr Pringle?" Mrs Walker from the school office was standing at the hall door waving a sheet of paper. "A word, please."

Mr Pringle frowned down at her. "Can't it wait?"

"I'm sorry, Mr Pringle. I think you'll want to hear this."

Mr Pringle trudged down the steps at the side of the stage. Mrs Walker whispered something in his ear and he trudged back up again.

Rosa turned round and signed to Leo, "Look at his face!"

Mr Pringle was doing something odd. It was like he was trying to laugh, talk and look serious at the same time. Finally, he gave a little cough.

"I'm sorry to say—" He squeezed the palm of his hand against his mouth and coughed again. "I'm sorry—" His voice seemed to squeak. Everyone in the hall leaned forward, including the teachers on stage. "I've just heard the tragic news that Nae Nae Juniors are no longer taking part in Dab's Best Blooms. Thank you."

He almost ran down the stairs and out of the hall. Leo couldn't be sure, but was that the sound of Pringle laughter? Miss Smith, the deputy head, stood up and started to dismiss the classes. Rosa was waiting for Leo in the corridor outside the hall.

She said, "Have you seen how many toads are outside?"

The window looked onto the junior playground. The wooden climbing frame was

covered in toads – twenty, maybe thirty of
them. As Leo and Rosa watched, Plum Pringle
ran out carrying the cat basket and stood in
the middle of the playground. She crouched
down and started fiddling with the straps.
Every single toad flopped off the frame and
landed next to her. Soon, she was in the middle
of a ring of toads.

Rosa looked at Leo in alarm. "Why's she doing that? Doesn't she know about Nigel?"

Leo thought about Mary Grimbow's cat, Nigel, on the *Frosty Morning* programme. He'd run away in terror as soon as he saw the toad.

"Here comes her dad," Leo said. "I think he's going to tell her to keep the cat in the basket so the toads don't get it."

Mr Pringle raced towards her, shouting and waving his hands. The toads didn't move. He snatched the basket off Plum, took her arm and hurried back into school. The toads sucked in their sides and even through the window Leo heard the trombone sound. More toads plopped onto the climbing frame. Within a few seconds, it was hard to see the wood beneath the pulsing, red-eyed creatures.

Leo shivered. "I hope they don't find a way in."

38

Chapter 5

Toads on the Roads

The toads found a way in. Mr Rib, the head cook, left the kitchen back door open to take out some rubbish. He came back to find a pair of toads paddling in his tray of beef stew.

When the Year 4 girls went to get ready for PE, the changing room had been taken over by a toad squad hopping from bench to bench. Toads perched on the windowsills outside and stared into the classrooms. No one could concentrate.

While Miss Quaver was pulling down the blinds, Rosa signed to Leo.

"I found out what happened to the Nae Nae garden."

He mouthed, "What?"

"Toads ate it."

They must have thought the bug hotel was lunch, with vegetables to go with it and fruit and flowers as pudding. No wonder Mr Pringle was laughing. His main rivals were gone.

News of the toad mob in the playground got round quickly. Worried families arrived early to pick up their children, meeting them by the toad-free staff entrance. It was hard for Rosa to lip read so many people at once, so Leo told her what people were saying.

He said, "Vespa's mum is furious because the toads ate all the baby apples. There won't be any apples to sell this September."

Rosa's eyes widened. "The toads ate a whole orchard?"

Leo nodded. "Abi's big sister is saying the toads went for their dog. Yan's mum saw the toads chasing a squirrel up a tree!"

Rosa said, "They've munched through Slide's musical garden too. I just saw Alex tell his grandma."

"I liked that garden," Leo said. "It wouldn't be fair if they keep the competition open after all this."

A van from the local builders' yard, Dab's Brick and Slab, pulled up in the staff car park. The builders opened the back doors of the van and pulled out long rolls of netting. They hoisted them on their shoulders and headed towards the nature garden.

Rosa said, "Mr Pringle will never give up!"

*

School was cancelled the next day. The toads wouldn't leave the playground and many of the families were having their own problems. There were reports of toads popping out of cereal boxes and getting stuck in car exhaust pipes. A toad even jumped through someone's window and landed next to them in the bath.

Rosa's Dad Ashley had to go to work, so she came to the shoe repair workshop with Leo. Everyone, including Maria from the shoe shop, was huddled round the laptop watching Dad Raj present his special edition of *Warts and All*. Behind him was a picture of a grand house.

"We are now sure that the toads in Upper Dab are Hunter gliding toads," Dad Raj said. "They started their lives here at Bog House. In Victorian times, it was owned by the Hunter family. Maddie Hunter and her husband were great animal collectors, and especially interested in toads and frogs."

The picture changed to a blurred black and white photo of a woman in a long skirt holding a frog in front of a pond.

"The Hunters collected frogs and toads from around the world. They also tried to breed their own. We now believe that Hunter gliding toads are part Wallace flying frog, part marsh frog and part cane toad."

Dad Raj's voice sank for the last two words. Leo wasn't surprised that Dad Raj had said that part quietly. When Mary Grimbow was on *Frosty Morning*, she'd said that cane toads eat everything.

The picture changed to a close-up of a Hunter gliding toad. *Was that Twerky again?* Leo thought.

"The Hunter gliding toads have big sticky toe pads so they can climb trees and walls. You can also see they have extra flaps of skin between their toes and more skin flaps between their legs and bodies. Even the sides of their bodies have extra skin, just like the flaps under plane wings. All this helps them glide."

"They open and close like umbrellas." Granddad sounded impressed.

Dad Raj pointed to a map. "We can now trace the toads' route from Bog House."

Yellow cartoon toads appeared on the map by a dot marked "Bog House". The toads moved across the map to another dot. The words "Nae Nae Juniors" flashed up underneath it.

"The toads stopped here for a while," Dad Raj said.

The map cut away to a picture of Nae Nae's garden. It wasn't really a garden any more. All Leo could see were a few stems and a leaf.

"Wow," Granddad said. "They must have been hungry."

"Look," Mum said. "They were still hungry when they left."

The TV was showing the map again. The yellow cartoon toads were moving towards another dot. They stopped.

Rosa read the caption underneath the dot. "Slide Music School."

"They ate that one too," Leo said.

Two more dots flashed up.

"That leaves Krump Middle School," Rosa said. "And Dab Juniors."

Leo said, "Even an elephant couldn't get through all the netting Mr Pringle's used. Our nature garden is safe from the toads."

"Shush," Mum said. "Raj hasn't finished yet."

"Thank you to everyone who contacted us with sightings of the toads before they reached Upper Dab," Dad Raj said. "I'm sorry that no one believed you at that time."

Mum pressed "pause" on the laptop. "We've had our first order from the Upper Dab Parks department. They want twenty Toad-Busters to protect their wardens. Three of them have been hit by toads and they're not happy."

"That's great news, Mum," said Leo. "You said the toads would be good for business."

"They're not great news for everybody," Granddad sighed.

"Stop being so gloomy," Mum said. "Loads of people love the toads. Tourists are coming from all over the country to see our toads. Dab Towers Hotel is fully booked for the first time in years. You know Elly Spenser, who runs the nature society? She's planning special toad walks. Lots of people have been very busy since the toads came."

Mum clicked onto a website selling Get Woke to the Croak stickers and notebooks. It even had a toad-themed recipe blog. Leo was pleased to see Toad Sundae was mainly made of mint choc chip ice cream, not real toad.

Mum and Granddad returned to making Toad-Busters. Maria went back to the shop. Leo and Rosa found a quiet corner behind some boxes of running shoes.

Rosa said, "Does your mum know about the Exploders?"

"The who?" Leo asked.

She showed Leo her phone. The Upper Dab Gardening Club website featured a video of a man wearing a T-shirt with a crow on it and the words "It's Time to Explode the Toads". "Cane toads are a pest!" the man in the crow

T-shirt said. "They won't rest until every cat, dog, squirrel and bird HAS BEEN EATEN!! Bring in the crows!"

"What's with the crows?" Leo asked.

Rosa made a face. "Some cane toads exploded in Germany a few years back. They think they were attacked by crows looking for food."

Leo frowned. "Why did the toads have to hide the crows' food?" he asked.

Rosa rolled her eyes. "The toads *were* the food," she said.

"Yuck! I wonder why the toads came here though," Leo said. "They could have chosen anywhere in the whole world, but they turned up in Upper Dab."

"Dad Raj has an idea but he's not saying until he's sure," Rosa replied.

"He likes to keep his secrets, doesn't he?"

"Yup," Rosa answered. "And there's another secret he's kept. He's a judge for the Dab's Best Blooms competition this year."

"Is it really going ahead?" Leo asked.

"Mr Pringle insisted."

Chapter 6

Toad Attack

Leo woke up to a cold drizzly Saturday. He peered out of his bedroom window. A trio of toads were huddled on top of the bus shelter. They bounced up to a low tree branch, caught a gust of wind and were gone. Leo craned his neck up.

The trio had joined a larger flock heading ... heading ...

Dad burst into the room holding Leo's phone. "It's all over the news! The toads have eaten the Krump Middle School garden and they're on their way to Dab Juniors! Rosa's just sent you a text. She's heading there now!"

Leo tumbled out of bed. "I'm on my way!"

*

Leo ran even faster than usual to school. Nae Nae Road was jammed with traffic. Leo spotted two outside-broadcast vans with their satellite dishes on their roofs. A minibus was parked on the pavement. An "Explode the Toad" banner was draped over the front seat. Cars were parked anywhere there was a space. Some of the windows were decorated with Exploders' crow logos, others with "Get Woke to the Croak" stickers. A wobbly line of toads bounced and flopped from car to car.

"Leo!" Rosa and Dad Ashley were waving at him from the other side of the road.

He ran over to them.

"Raj and the other judges are in there now," Dad Ashley said. "And so is half the town."

"Excuse me, please!" A man in a dark suit and sunglasses nudged past them. A cage swung from his hand. Inside it, a large black bird stretched its wings and cawed.

Dad Ashley touched Rosa's shoulder and signed "crow".

Rosa clapped her hand to her mouth. "That means they really are going to explode the toads! We have to do something!"

They ran around the back to the junior playground. The climbing frame was empty.

Leo said, "Where have the toads gone?"

"Up there," Rosa said.

She was right. Rows and rows of toads were sitting on the roof. It reminded Leo of class visits to the swimming pool when everyone was sitting on the edge, waiting for their turn to jump in.

Somewhere from the front of the nature garden, Mr Pringle's voice echoed through a microphone. "I am absolutely delighted—"

He was drowned out by shouts of "Explode the toads! Explode the toads!"

Leo, Rosa and Dad Ashley hurried round to the nature garden gates. It was impossible to see inside. A dense crowd of people spilled out into the playground. They were waving banners with pictures of crows.

Dad Ashley tapped his phone. "I've texted Raj."

Rosa shook her head. "He's not going to look at his phone at the moment," she said.

"Excuse me, please." The man with the
crow had caught up with them. A woman at
the back of the crowd turned round, saw the
crow and smiled. She tapped the shoulder of
the man in front of her and a path opened up
ahead into the garden. Rosa and Leo sneaked
through.

The netting had been rolled aside and even in the drizzle the garden looked glorious. Mr Pringle was standing on a low wooden stage. Sitting behind him was Dad Raj, the Dab mayor, wearing a massive chain around her neck, and an older man wearing wellies and a red tracksuit.

"That's Ivan Stitch," Rosa whispered. "He writes about gardening for the *Dab Daily*."

Ivan Stitch stepped forward. He was holding a gold cup. Mr Pringle was smiling so hard it looked like his chin might fall off.

"I can't believe it," Leo said. "How can we win a competition if there's nobody else in it?"

"Plum Pringle doesn't look happy neither," Rosa said.

Plum had crept onto the stage and was sitting in Ivan's seat. The cat basket was by her feet. A toad flopped onto a pot of strawberry plants. Mr Pringle's eyes twitched towards it. He frowned, turned around and saw Plum. He made a little sign with his hands, as if he wanted her to go away. Instead, she picked up the cat basket, stood up and walked towards the centre of the stage. The crow in the cage cawed loudly.

The cat inside the basket replied with its strange trombone sound.

Leo nudged Rosa. "It's making that noise again."

Plum stood next to Mr Pringle. Two toads landed next to her.

Mr Pringle tried to wave her away again. "Plum! Go back to your seat!" he whispered.

"No!" She grabbed the microphone from her father. "I think everybody has a right to know why the toads are here!"

"Plum!" Mr Pringle reached over to grab the mic back, but a real toad thumped down onto his shoulder.

Plum carried on. "My brother, Aspen, is a gardener at Bog House. He told Dad about these toads he'd spotted in a pond in their grounds. He thought it was funny that they climbed trees, but he also told Dad they loved eating snails and slugs. He said they would be perfect for our nature garden. He brought us one, but then all its friends followed."

Dad Raj's eyes widened. His mouth moved.

Rosa signed, "Dad Raj just said it's the queen."

"The queen?" Leo said. "Are you sure?"

Plum held the carrier up. "Now all its friends want it back. I've told Dad that it's cruel to keep it!"

"Queen?" Rosa frowned at Leo. "Of course! Queen, like a queen bee! She's the one that all the other toads follow. Stupid Aspen stole the most important toad in the pond!"

"Explode the Toads!"

Leo looked round to see the banners waving wildly. The crow jumped up and down, making its cage shake.

The mayor screeched. A toad had plopped onto her head and then bounced across the stage. She ran off into the crowd, almost overtaken by Ivan Stitch.

Plum Pringle began to undo one of the basket straps. "It's OK, toads. You can have your friend back now."

The straps were loose, but before Plum could open the lid, Mary Grimbow pushed through the crowd and grabbed the basket.

"Gotcha!" she cried. She waved the basket towards the man with the crow. "If you take this one, all the others will come after it." She held the basket above her head like she'd been given her own prize. "Let's go and do some exploding!"

"Oh no you don't!" someone said from behind her. It was Dad Raj.

He tried to grab the basket, but the toads got there first. With a blast of booming battle croaks, the toad troop stormed in. They swooped, hopped and leaped, a bellowing mass of yellow skin, red eyes and flicking tongues. They hit the stage with a sound like a wet sponge slapping a wall.

Mary Grimbow dropped the basket. The lid flapped open and something leaped out. Dad Raj jumped up and caught it.

"I've got her!" Dad Raj called. "We need to get her out of here!"

"Release the crow!" Mary Grimbow yelled into the crowd. "Release—" A toad bounced onto her forehead and stuck there. "Get off!" she shouted.

The stage was a mass of toads. Mr Pringle was telling Plum off, but she was smiling and ignoring him. Mary Grimbow was still yelling, but now the toads were turning their attention to Dad Raj.

"Take her somewhere safe!" Dad Raj shouted as the other toads plopped and glided towards him.

He threw the queen toad. She skimmed through the air and before she had a chance to glide away, Rosa caught her. Leo glanced to his side. The man in the sunshades was bending over the crow cage. It looked like he was opening the door.

"Quick!" Leo said.

Side by side, they tried to push their way through the crowds, but it was impossible. The toads were following, their giant toe pads using people's heads like trampolines. Leo and Rosa were getting bashed about as people tried to unstick the toads. The toad in Rosa's hands called harder. More toads massed around them.

Mary Grimbow must have grabbed the microphone. "Yes! The crow has been released!"

"We can't do it!" Rosa was close to tears. "We can't save them!"

"Leo! Over here!" Was that Mum? Leo stood on tip toe. It sounded like her, but he couldn't see her. Then a big red umbrella popped up. And a rainbow one next to it. Both had bright Dolly's Brollies logos printed across them.

"It's Mum and Granddad! Rosa, give the toad to me!" Leo shouted.

"What?"

"Trust me!" he said.

Rosa handed over the toad. It blinked up at him and tooted. Then Leo threw her forward with all his strength. The queen toad sped through the air, thudded against the red umbrella, shot up, dropped down onto the rainbow umbrella and flipped away.

RELEASE THE CROWS!

"Got her!" came Dad Ashley's voice from the back of the crowd.

*

Rosa went back to the workshop with Leo's family to watch the queen's journey. A news helicopter was filming the swarm of toads as they followed Dad Ashley's car along the quiet country back roads. They were heading to a reptile sanctuary owned by one of Dad Raj's friends.

Rosa said, "They'll probably end up back at Bog House, but they'll need a special pond enclosure."

"That's a bit sad," Leo said. "Before Aspen stole the queen, they weren't bothering anyone."

"I know. But it's to protect them too. There are still lots of angry Exploders out there."

Mum beckoned them over to the laptop. "You two! Look! We're famous!"

Photos of the toad bouncing from umbrella to umbrella had been shared hundreds of times. Everyone wanted to know where they could get the brollies that made perfect toad trampolines.

"We need to set up a website," Granddad said.

"I'll ask Dad Ashley," Rosa said. "He's almost as good at making websites as he is at catching toads."

Mum scrolled through the photos. The last one was taken at Dab Juniors. There was Mr Pringle standing in the middle of the nature garden. Except the nature garden was all munched up, and all the plants and pots had been knocked down. Plum Pringle stood next to him. She was holding his hand and offering him a packet of seeds.

Rosa looked at Leo. "Do you think Mr Pringle will try again next year?" she asked.

"Yes," Leo said. "But I think he'll check the sky for flying toads first."